The Parrot Tico Tango

written and illustrated by

Anna Witte

Barefoot Books
Celebrating Art and Story

The parrot Tico Tango
Had a round, **yellow** mango,

But it wasn't quite as yellow
As the lemon of Marcello.

And Tico Tango knew
That he had to have it too,
So he took it!

The parrot Tico Tango
Had a round, yellow mango,

And he carried to his right
A lemon small and bright,

When he spied Elena's fig,
Which was **purple**, sweet and big.

And Tico Tango knew
That he had to have it too,
So he grabbed it!

The parrot Tico Tango
Had a round, yellow mango,

And he carried to his right
A lemon small and bright,

And on his left, a fig,
Which was purple, sweet and big,

When he noticed his friend Terry
With a **red**, juicy cherry.

And Tico Tango knew
That he had to have it too,
So he stole it!

The parrot Tico Tango
Had a round, yellow mango,

And he carried to his right
A lemon small and bright,

And on his left, a fig,
Which was purple, sweet and big,

And on his back, from Terry,
A red, juicy cherry,

When he saw Marina munch
On a **green** grape bunch.

And Tico Tango knew
That he had to have it too,
So he snatched it!

The parrot Tico Tango
Had a round, yellow mango,

And he carried to his right
A lemon small and bright,

And on his left, a fig,
Which was purple, sweet and big,

And on his back, from Terry,
A red, juicy cherry,

And he clutched the grapes he'd put
In his strong sharp foot,

When he spotted proud Soraya
With a deep **orange** papaya.

And Tico Tango knew
That he had to have it too,
So he seized it!

The parrot Tico Tango
Had a round, yellow mango,

And he carried to his right
A lemon small and bright,

And on his left, a fig,
Which was purple, sweet and big,

And on his back, from Terry,
A red, juicy cherry,

And he clutched the grapes he'd put
In his strong sharp foot,

And in his other foot he held
The papaya he had smelled,

When he saw his good friend Nate
With a tiny, **brown** date.

And Tico Tango knew
That he had to have it too!

So he opened his beak wide

To fit it deep inside, when ...

Down came
the cherry!

Down came
the grapes!

And down came
the papaya!

POOR TICO TANGO!

Now, the parrot Tico Tango
Didn't even have his mango!

But his friends thought: what a treat!
All that fruit they had to eat!

They took the fruit he stole
And they put it in a bowl,

They washed it and they sliced it,
They peeled it and they diced it.

Tico Tango felt contrite.
He knew he had to put things right.

"Please forgive me, I feel bad
That I took the fruit you had."

And the parrot Tico Tango
Begged for just one piece of mango.

His friends were quite divided,
But soon they all decided

He deserved another chance:
They would make the parrot dance!

"If you teach us all to tango
You can have a piece of mango!"

And Tico Tango knew
That he had to have it too,

So he danced for it!

For Alex,

with whom I ran barefoot along a beach in southern Costa Rica,
where we first saw Tico Tango...

Barefoot Books
2067 Massachusetts Ave
Cambridge, MA 02140

This book was typeset in Sassoon Primary and Flora
The illustrations were prepared in fabrics,
acrylic paint, paper, ink and pastels

Graphic design by Barefoot Books, England
Color separation by Grafiscan, Italy
Printed and bound in Singapore by Tien Wah Press Pte Ltd

This book has been printed on 100% acid-free paper

Library of Congress Cataloging-in-Publication Data

Witte, Anna.
The parrot Tico Tango / written and illustrated by Anna Witte.
    p. cm.
  Summary: A cumulative rhyme in which a greedy parrot keeps taking fruit from the other creatures
of the rainforest until he can hold no more.
   ISBN 1-84148-243-9
   [1. Parrots--Fiction. 2. Greed--Fiction. 3. Rain forest animals--Fiction. 4. Stories in rhyme.] I. Title.
PZ8.3.W765Par 2004
   [E]--dc22

                        2004004656

                  1 3 5 7 9 8 6 4 2

Barefoot Books
Celebrating Art and Story

At Barefoot Books, we celebrate art and story with books that open the
hearts and minds of children from all walks of life, inspiring them to read deeper,
search further, and explore their own creative gifts. Taking our inspiration from many
different cultures, we focus on themes that encourage independence of spirit,
enthusiasm for learning, and acceptance of other traditions. Thoughtfully prepared
by writers, artists and storytellers from all over the world, our products combine
the best of the present with the best of the past to educate our children
as the caretakers of tomorrow.

www.barefootbooks.com